Two mischievous children romp through the week,
causing chaos everywhere. But then, on Friday,
something funny happens and they become
mysteriously quiet and well behaved . . .

For Julie, Jemma and Lauren

On Friday something funny happened

John Prater

PUFFIN BOOKS

On Saturday we went shopping.

On Sunday
we went to the park.

On Monday
we did the washing.

On Tuesday Uncle John came to lunch.

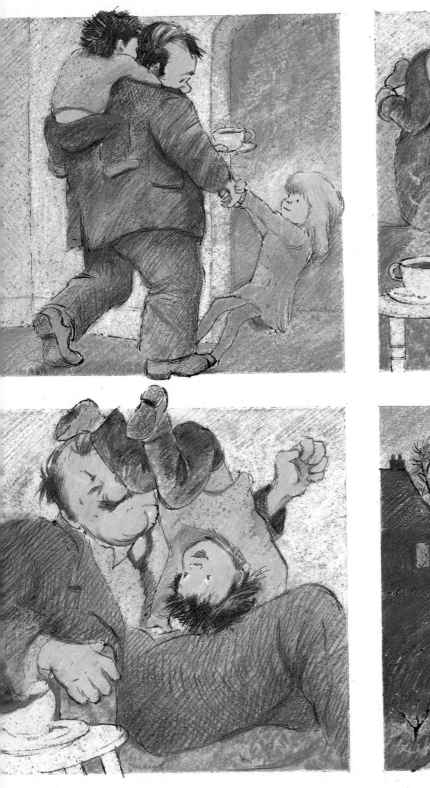

On Wednesday
we did some painting.

On Thursday we played with our friends.

On Friday something
funny happened—
and the house was
very quiet.

On Saturday
we went shopping . . .